The Ghost

of

Christmas

to

Come

by D. P. Conway

Part of
The Christmas Collection

Day Lights Publishing House, Inc.
Cleveland Ohio

From Darkness to Light through the Power of Story

The Christmas Collection

Go to Series Page on Amazon

or

Search DP Conway Books

Did you receive this as a gift? Please post a review on
AmazonYou can reach Dan at authordpconway@gmail.com

Dedications

For Marisa
Thanks for allowing me to follow my passion.

For my biggest fans, my children,
Colleen, Bridget, Patrick, and Christopher.

And for my "can't miss" future biggest fans,
my little Aubrey
and my little Avery.

Contents

Chapter 1

Outskirts of Boston, Massachusetts
Winter

1953

"Matty, wakeup. It's time to go home."

Matty opened her tired old eyes to look once again at the man. She knew who he was. He came often and usually asked her the same question. She usually gave the same answer, too. "My home is here with them."

"But they are not there, Matty. I've told you that." The man had tried to convince her of this for longer than she could remember.

She raised her eyebrows at him, then glanced out the window to the distant Cemetery Hill. "Oh, yes, they are. Their names are all written there. Etched in stone. So, don't try to trick me."

He sighed, "Oh, Matty. I wish you would believe me."

"Go away. I don't want to talk to you today."

The man sighed again, louder this time. He let himself out the same way he had come in. He would visit another day.

Matty watched him leave, then stared at the ceiling for a while, wondering what day it was. Though she had been cross with him this morning, she was glad the man came to visit her. No one else ever did. Without him, she would have no one.

The sound of voices outside the window disrupted her thoughts. Her brow furrowed, and her lips clenched as she threw her blanket off the edge of the bed and swung her feet over the side onto the floor. *Ugg.* She winced. Every part of her body ached this morning, like it did most mornings. She reached behind herself and held her back with one hand, then slowly stood up and hobbled a few short steps to the upstairs bedroom window. They were there all right, the neighborhood riff-raff who came to use their sleds to ride down the hill at the side of her house.

There was a large hill on her property, one that the neighborhood kids had decided would be perfect for sledding in the long winter months that were common in this area of Massachusetts. She lived in a town on the outskirts of Boston. Her house was the last house on a street that stretched along a ridge right before dipping into the valley. On the other side of the valley was Cemetery Hill, which rose even higher than the hill her house was on, and just as steeply.

Matty, as her family had called her from a young age, had lived here her whole life. All her family had been born here and died here. They were all since passed and laid to rest up there, in the cemetery across the valley, at the top of Cemetery Hill.

Cemetery Hill had been looking down over the town for over 200 years. It sat at the farthest edge and was a few acres in size with large old oak trees, planted long ago by the town's founders, surrounding the entire perimeter. A single zig-zag, winding road led from the base of the valley up to the cemetery. The road had been built that way in the old days, so wagons and teams of horses could zig-zag their way up the hill when pulling the newest occupants of the cemetery during the often-inclement Massachusetts weather.

The road circled the perimeter at the top, running just inside the oak trees, leaving room for graves to either side. At the very back, looking down upon all the graves, and the distant village as well, stood a fifteen-foot-tall weathered cross made of sculptured stone and bearing the image of Jesus. A famous sculptor had put it up there some eighty years earlier because his wife had died. Matty didn't know her, or him for that matter. She only knew the story.

The ground below the cross was considered the most sacred on Cemetery Hill, as several of the early town priests and ministers were buried there. In the old days, everyone was buried up there.

There were over three hundred gravestones in the cemetery, many of them family gravestones, from families long gone from the village's landscape and memory. The place had mostly filled up and was becoming more of a historic site than anything else.

Matty's home was a run-down old farmhouse with weathered white wooden siding and faded green shutters. A slate stone walk led from the sidewalk to worn stone steps, which ascended onto a large rickety porch made of thin gray wooden floorboards, also faded by time. It had two stories: a modest front room, dining room, and a small kitchen on the first floor, and three small bedrooms upstairs. Like the cemetery, her house too had once looked over the town and had once been the only house on the street. But modern progress had taken away its solitude. Now, there was an entire street of houses, all close together, and her house's prominence had long since passed.

Matty watched the kids sledding for a moment, lamenting they had not heeded her warning from last time. She put on her old blue cotton robe and fumbled with her frail fingers to tie it around her waist. She slipped on her house slippers, then slowly walked around the bed, passing her dresser mirror. She stopped to catch a disappointing glimpse of her gray hair and wrinkled skin, then, not wanting to see herself anymore, headed into the cold hall and down the creaky old stairs. She crossed the aged wooden floor of the living room and went to the door.

She opened the door and unexpectedly inhaled an immediate dose of the early December air as the wind whistled through her robe, causing her whole body to shiver. It had snowed again last night, and there was now a good five inches on the ground, including two fresh inches on her steps and the front half of her porch.

Trying not to slip on the freshly fallen snow, she carefully walked to the side of the porch where she could get a better glimpse of the kids. She held onto the old white post holding up the porch roof and shouted, "Hey, you kids! I told you before! Get out of my yard!"

"Ahhhh!" one yelled. "It's old lady Mattyton!" screamed another. "Run!" came the collective shriek of the children. Two took off down the hill on their sleds while the other three ran toward the front of the house.

"I told you to stay out of here!" Matty yelled, the shriek of her old crackly voice surprising herself, as the frightened children ran off. She added, "I'll summon the sheriff next time!" She could hear them laughing in the distance as they all disappeared. She tried to shrug off the sound of their laughter, but she knew it would be ringing in her ears until bedtime, and this scared her.

Chapter 2

Matty went inside, sat down in her living room chair, and began to rock. Her eyes were sullen, drooping. Her hands were trembling, and her mouth hung open some. She closed her eyes, shuddering, slowing her breath, trying to calm her racing heart. Children scared her. They had frightened her for a very long time. She could not remember why they frightened her, but they did. Finally, she collected herself, vowing she would get through this day and go to bed early.

Her rocking chair sat next to the window that looked to the west, toward Cemetery Hill. It was a sturdy wooden rocker that her husband George had bought for her when she had been expecting their first child, little George. It was made of oak and stained with cherry wood stain. There was a cushion on it, and every day, she would sit in this chair for hours, gently rocking, thinking about her life gone by, once in a while looking up at the cemetery where her family was all laid to rest. In the evenings, when the sun was setting, the warm rays would shine through the window onto her face, giving her hope for another day.

The rest of the day passed slowly, as usual. When the sun finally set, as it did early in this darkening time of the year, she went up the staircase and down the hall past the two bedrooms they had never used to her room at the end of the hall.

Matty's room had one dresser and a dark oak framed double bed. It never felt like a large room when George was alive, but now that he was gone, it felt expansive and empty. There were two windows, one facing the cemetery, the other looking out over an old farmland field that separated her street from a nearby neighborhood.

Matty put on her nightgown and was under the covers before dusk settled into darkness. As usual, she fell asleep within a short time. She slept peacefully, thankful she did after another long and tedious day by herself.

The following morning when she woke, the man was there again. He said cheerfully, "Matty, wake up. Are you ready to go?"

"NO! I told you!" She spoke forcefully this time, in a high pitched tone, and it surprised her. She did not normally grow this angry with him. She opened her eyes and saw the frown on his face. His thick brown hair hung over his brown eyes as he looked down at his folded hands, as though he didn't know what to do.

Matty felt terrible for scolding him. She cleared her dry throat and said in a remorseful voice, "Go home, now. I'm sorry for being cross."

He smiled and gently patted her on the shoulder, "It's OK, Matty."

She shook her head, turned over, and went back to sleep.

The children did not come today, and she was glad. She could not bear the thought of another long day enduring their shouts and laughs in her mind. More than that, she did not like them tearing up the landscape with their red flyer sleds. It made her view out to Cemetery Hill look tarnished and dirty. She laid in bed for a long while, then lifted her blanket and swung her feet onto the floor. In the distance, she could see the barren oak trees on top of Cemetery Hill swaying in the late December breeze. It reminded her of her own life, so very barren now, with no leaves to speak of, reeling in an endless cold wind, waiting for what, she did not know.

She stood up and labored to go downstairs, then sat in her rocking chair, thinking about her husband George. She had met him at a dance when she was just eighteen. George was a dashing young man from Boston three years older than her. He had arrow-straight black hair, which he always parted neatly to the left, and kind blue eyes that glistened when he smiled at her. When she met him, he had just finished college in Boston and graduated as an engineer. They fell in love, got married within the year, and moved to this house which had been given to Matty by her grandmother.

She thought back to all the beautiful days she and George had at the house. She thought about all the love they had shared and all the dances they had driven into town to attend. She thought of the friends they had, the wonderful friends who shared their passion for dancing and going into town for ice cream or to catch a play at the theater.

But that was before the hard years had come. These were years she could not talk about anymore, not to anyone. The man who visited her wanted to talk about them and often tried to bring them up, but she would not. Those years were the reason she was stuck. They were the reason that this place was still her home now. She glanced out the window, up at the cemetery, and wiped away a lone tear that rolled down her cheek. and wiped away a lone tear that rolled down her cheek.

The day passed particularly slowly, but that evening, as the sun was setting over the cemetery, illuminating her face as it often did, she felt a tinge of hope she had not felt in a very long time. She didn't know why, but the sun on her face felt more wonderful than she ever remembered. It occurred to her that she had not felt this way since before the hard years had come. The feeling startled her, causing her to notice how profound the absence of this hope had been. She sat still, relishing the rays of the sun, trying to remember more about the days before the hard years took over her life until finally, the sun disappeared behind barren oak trees and the horizon of the cemetery. She sighed, got up slowly, and lumbered up the staircase, getting into bed before darkness came.

Chapter 3

The next morning, she was awakened by the noise of the neighborhood kids. They were back. She tightened her lip and grimaced, then threw off her blanket and swung her feet off the bed. She put on her old blue cotton robe, tying it at the waist, and put on her slippers. She wasn't feeling the usual pains today and was surprised. Feeling stronger than she had in a very long time, she marched down the hall at a steady pace. She went down the stairs and over to the door and opened it, expecting a rush of cold air, but none came. It was cold though, bitter cold, the kind of cold that hangs like a blanket in the air.

No fresh snow had fallen, and the snow and ice on the lawn and walks shimmered in the faint morning light. She stepped out onto the porch and carefully walked across to the other side. There were five children there today, the same bunch, give or take, that usually came.

She trembled, slowly gathering her courage, then cried out, "Hey, you kids! Get out of my yard! I told you I'd summon the sheriff next time!"

"Old lady Mattyton!" one yelled, and they all screamed, then instantly scattered, two heading to the back and three others heading to the front. One girl, who looked like the youngest, ran toward the front screaming, but she slipped and fell hard, hitting her face on the sidewalk.

"Oh my," Matty said, looking down from the porch at the girl sprawled out, face down, on the icy sidewalk in front of her house.

The girl was bundled in a purple snowsuit with a pink hat, pink scarf, and matching gloves. She was not moving. She laid still no more than twenty feet from Matty. The little girl's friends were in the distance now, and Matty realized they had not seen her fall. Matty thought of calling out to stop them, to tell them to come back, but they were too far for her feeble voice to reach them. Then, all at once, the girl started to cry.

Matty rocked back and forth, looking down, unsure what to do. She called out, "Hey, hey, are... are you all right?"

But the girl only kept crying, increasing in intensity every few seconds. She looked to be no more than seven or eight years old by the size of her. Her crying grew louder, causing Matty to panic. She could see a trickle of blood on the little girl's face.

Matty looked down at her slippers as if looking could command them to move. They wanted to go help, but neither she nor they had been off the porch in many, many years. *I have to help her.* She thought.

She walked over to the steps, gingerly took hold of the rail, and stepped down slowly, step by step, until her foot reached out and touched the ground. She was afraid to put her full weight on it and instead just felt the cold ground for a few moments, making sure it was solid enough to hold her.

Finally, she put her foot down and then followed with the other foot. She looked down at her slippers again. She could not remember the last time she had been off the porch. She trembled, and thought of turning right around and going back inside. She looked up, still holding the very end of the porch railing, unwilling to let go. The girl was still sobbing loudly, only fifteen feet or so away.

Matty looked at the pathway in front of her, assessing the risk. The walks were cleanly shoveled, and she imagined the man had done it. He usually did, for his own traversing of them, as she would never use them, but today, she had to. She slowly walked down her entrance walk to the sidewalk, then turned and went over to the girl. She was naturally hesitant to get too near. She leaned forward a bit, not wanting to step too close and asked, "Are you OK?"

But the girl's incessant crying only heightened. Matty drew a step closer now, then leaned forward more, putting her hands on her knees this time. In a voice growing more worried by the moment, she asked, "Are you OK, little girl?"

But the girl kept crying. Matty could now see the trickle of blood had reached the sidewalk and stained the snow red. She leaned closer, trying to get a look at the girl's face, not sure what to do, not sure how bad it was. The girl needed help, though, and she could not leave her. Matty looked around. No one else was in sight, and it was eerily quiet except for the girl's crying. It was up to her. She leaned forward again and said in a frail but kind voice, "Come, little girl. Let me help you up."

The girl's crying paused for a moment, and she turned her head sideways to peer up at Matty. Matty could see her rosy red cheeks and reddened nose with blood running out. The girl had hit her nose hard. Matty felt sorry for her and reached out her wrinkled hand. The girl lumbered up onto her hands and knees but kept sobbing. She glanced up slightly again, then took Matty's hand. Matty felt a shiver run up her spine, the age-old warning she always felt around children, but it only lasted for a moment this time. The girl needed her help, and she had to put her fears aside.

Matty helped the girl to stand and saw that she had beautiful blonde hair and an Angelic face with large blue eyes. The girl's eyes met Matty's for a moment, but she kept crying, holding her gloved hands to her nose. Matty said, "Oh, your face is all blood. I think you hurt your nose."

The girl looked up, and between heaving sobs, said, "It hurts."

"Come with me," Matty said, "I'll get a towel from the house and help you get cleaned up."

Matty took the girl's hand and led her along the shoveled walks and up the stairs onto the porch. She opened the creaky storm door, and they stepped inside. The girl stood inside the doorway, not sure what to do until Matty pointed to a chair by the door and said, "You sit here. I'll go get a towel."

Matty slowly walked across the wooden floor, scanning the sparsely furnished home, and suddenly her eyes widened. There was an old towel she had not noticed in years sitting behind an old lamp on the end table. She smiled, picked it up, went over to the kitchen sink, and turned the handle. Water came out, and she sighed with relief, dampening the old towel.

She went back into the front room. The girl had stopped crying and was holding her bloodied gloves to her nose. Matty bent down in front of her and helped the girl untie her hood and gently lifted it back. She slowly removed the girl's hat and gloves, then gently cleaned the blood off the girl's face and coat.

Matty was proud of herself. She stood up straight, admiring her handiwork, feeling stronger than she had in a very long time and said, "You better go home now."

The girl sniffled again and asked in a needy tone, "Can you call my mom?"

Matty replied hesitantly, "I… I don't know how."

The girl asked again. "Can you call my mom?"

Matty felt unsure of herself. She fumbled her words, saying in a quiet voice, "No, I don't know how to do that. Now, where… where do you live?"

"Over there," the girl said, pointing out the door to the neighborhood beyond the old farm field, in the opposite direction of Cemetery Hill.

"What's your name?" asked Matty, her face muscles tightening some as she began to feel anxious.

"Aubrey," the girl replied shyly.

Matty said, gingerly, "Well, go home, Aubrey. Your momma can help you, now that you're all cleaned up and able to walk."

"OK, thank you," the girl said as she slid off the chair. Matty helped the girl put her hat back on and tucked her gloves into the coat pockets. She then opened the storm door and let the girl out. She watched her walk down the sidewalk and cross over the field. Matty waited until she was out of sight, then shut the door. She went to her rocking chair and began to shiver and tremble. A feeling of fear swept through her. She rocked and rocked, trying to breathe, trying to slow her racing heart. Finally, the sun began to set, and after it did, a feeling of calm returned to her, and she went up to bed.

Chapter 4

The next morning Matty heard the man's kind voice whisper, "Matty, it's time to wake up."

She frowned, opened her tired eyes, and asked, "What do you want?"

He replied, "Nothing important, Matty. Do you need anything?"

Matty answered with subtle defiance, "No, I do not."

The man smiled. He then raised his chin some and said, "I see you had a visitor yesterday."

Matty narrowed her eyes, and raised her finger from beneath the blanket, pointing at him. "Yes, I did. And that's none of your business. Now go away."

The man replied, patiently asking, "Do you want to come with me today?"

"No! I told you." She rolled over to face away from him.

The man then left, saying, "Have a good day, Matty."

~ ~ ~ ~

An hour later, there was a knock at the front door. Matty sat up, her eyes wide, her face muscles tightening. No one ever came to her door. She hesitated, listening. Perhaps she had imagined it. There was another knock. She threw off her blanket, swung her feet onto the floor, and stood up, then took a few steps to look out the window. There was a long light-blue car parked in front of her old mailbox at the end of her driveway. It looked like one of the Buicks George had wanted to buy. It looked to be a brand new one.

Matty put on her old blue cotton robe, feebly tied it at the waist, put her on her slippers, went down the hall and down the stairs.

The knock came again, louder this time. She reached the door, slightly short of breath, and with trembling hands, grasped the doorknob and opened it. A woman looking to be around thirty, with fair skin, freckles, and long brown hair, stood straight and tall, holding a basket in her hand. Next to her was Aubrey, whose nose was bandaged with white gauze and looked slightly bruised. On the other side of the woman was a younger girl, perhaps six or seven years old. Matty looked at them through the storm door glass for a few moments, unsure of what to do.

The woman smiled and gestured for her to open the door, so she did.

"Hi," Matty said, in a weak, timid voice.

The woman warmly and replied, "I am sorry to bother you. I am Aubrey's mom. She said you helped her yesterday, and I wanted to thank you."

Matty smiled, and her body tensed up as her trembling hand held tightly to the slightly propped door.

The woman extended her hand and said, "My name is Colleen Cooper. You've already met Aubrey, and this is her sister Avery."

Matty looked slowly into each of the two little girl's faces. They were both smiling. Neither of them seemed to be afraid of her. She reached out her hand and timidly shook the woman's hand, keeping the door only partially opened, and said in a feeble voice, "It's nice to meet you."

The woman responded, asking, "What is your name?"

Matty was taken aback for a moment, "Me?" she asked. "My name is… Elizabeth… Elizabeth Korza…" she paused, "but they used to call me Matty."

The woman smiled and glanced down at the basket in her hands and said, "It's nice to meet you, Matty. I hope you don't mind, but we made you some nut bread."

Matty looked down at the small basket with something inside it. She opened the door wider and accepted the basket, saying, "Thank you."

The woman replied cheerfully, "You're welcome," then she asked, "Do you live here alone?"

Matty hesitated, she wasn't used to talking with anyone other than the man. She replied, "Uhh, yes, I do. I've been alone for some time now."

The woman glanced back at the perfectly shoveled walkway, and asked, "Who takes such good care of your walks?"

Matty leaned over and looked at the cleared pathway and replied, "There is a man who comes. I imagine he does it."

The woman looked back at Matty, and said, "That's very nice of him." She took her girl's hands and said, "It was nice to meet you, Matty, and thank you again for helping Aubrey."

Matty smiled, wider this time, and said, "You're welcome," then closed the door.

Chapter 5

The days were growing very short now. Matty had no clocks or calendars in her home and had learned to rely solely on her skill at gauging the time and the seasons by the rising and setting sun. The short days meant that Christmas was drawing near.

She laid awake for a while, then got up and finally made her way downstairs when she heard them again. It was the neighborhood kids. She put on her robe and slippers and walked out onto the porch. There they were alright, all five of them, with two sleds, going down the hill and marching back up, making quite a mess of things. Matty started to shout out, then stopped. The little girl Aubrey was with them, her nose still bandaged. There was a broad smile on the young girl's face, peeking out from behind her bandage. Matty observed them for a few moments, then went inside.

She sat in her rocking chair, slowly moving back and forth, looking out beyond the children, up onto Cemetery Hill. Periodically, she sat up taller in her chair, watching the children again, paying particular attention to the girl Aubrey, who was laughing and smiling and having fun.

Matty kept rocking and watching until the children had long left, then sat still, waiting for the sunset to come. Once the sun had set behind the cemetery horizon, she went up to bed.

~ ~ ~ ~

The following morning, the man did not come, and Matty wondered why. She laid awake in bed for a long time, thinking about the little girls, Aubrey and Avery. She was glad they had come to her house. She was glad they had not been afraid of her, and for some reason that she did not understand, she had not been afraid of them either.

The next day, around midday, there was a knock at her door. Matty got up from her rocker and walked over to the front door, and opened it. It was the woman and her two daughters again. Behind them, parked by her old mailbox, was their light blue car.

"Hi, Matty," said Colleen. "I hope you don't mind us stopping by. The girls and I wanted to ask you something."

Matty replied, tentatively, keeping the door only slightly ajar, "Oh, what would that be?"

The woman looked down at Aubrey, prompting her. Aubrey smiled with anticipation, then turned to Matty and asked, "Will you come and have dinner with us on Christmas Eve?"

Matty felt a tinge of fear race up her spine, "I... I... don't know. I have not... gone out in a very long time."

Colleen replied without hesitation, "Well, we can pick you up, and we can bring you home, too."

Matty looked down at her faded blue cotton robe and said, "But I don't know what to wear?"

Colleen smiled and replied in a hopeful tone, "You can wear anything you like."

Matty thought for a moment, with her eyebrows furrowed, trying to decide. She remembered seeing some dresses hanging in the closet in her room. Perhaps she might wear one of those.

Aubrey interrupted her thoughts, "Will you come?"

Matty looked down at the girl's pretty blond hair and big blue eyes set back behind her slightly bruised nose. The girl was not afraid of her, which made Matty happy, something she had not felt in a very long time. Matty looked over at the other girl, Avery, quietly leaning against her mother's leg, waiting for Matty to answer. She was not afraid either.

Matty awkwardly smiled, and cleared her throat, then said, "I will come. When is it?"

Colleen replied, "Tomorrow evening. My husband and Aubrey will come and pick you up at 4:30."

"OK, thank you," Matty said as she quietly closed the door.

Chapter 6

The next day Matty woke with a small smile on her face, feeling a surge of hope she had not felt in ages. She got up out of bed without her usual aches and pains and went over to the closet, a closet she had not opened in many, many years. She marveled at what was inside and counted seven dresses, mostly flower-patterned, all hung neatly in a row.

Matty remembered them now. The white one with the blue flower pattern had always been her favorite. She put it on and went to the mirror. What she saw surprised her. She had grown very old since the last time she had donned this dress. Her skin was wrinkled and sagging, and her hair was white and messy. Her eyes, once deep brown with dark brows and lashes, were now more grayish, and her eyebrows just as gray. She looked down at her legs below the hemline. They were once vivacious and muscular, but now, they were thin, wrinkled, and slightly swollen at the ankles.

Matty sighed, recalling that she had once been young and full of life. Now, taking the time to see herself in the mirror, she felt like a shell of what she had once been.

She walked back over to the closet and took out a pair of white shoes with a low heel. She slipped them on and went downstairs to sit in her rocker and wait.

The day passed slowly. She spent most of it looking out at Cemetery Hill, remembering George, remembering her friends. She thought of her mother, too, long since gone. She was up there in that cemetery. Matty missed her mother, perhaps more than anyone. She had been an immigrant from Hungary and worked part-time at the local Church cleaning the rectory to help make ends meet. She had died when Matty was only a newlywed, and because of it, had not been there for the hard years. Matty lamented this fact, for her mother perhaps could have helped her, perhaps even saved some of… she stopped. George had always told her there was no use in wishing for things that God alone was in charge of. Still, she believed her mother could have helped her.

Matty's thoughts then turned to Christmas. "So, it's Christmas Eve," she said to herself. "Mother always told us magical things happen on Christmas Eve." It was indeed a magical night. It seemed on that night, of all nights, Heaven became one with the Earth. You could reach out and touch the feeling in the air. Before the hard years came, she and George relished Christmas Eve, often spending it with friends and family, and sometimes just the two of them, but it was always special.

It occurred to Matty that it had been many years since she had remembered Christmas. She realized many Christmas Eves had probably come and gone over the last, however many years, without her even noticing. Before the hard years, while George was alive, she had always imagined Christmas Eve in their home, with all the children, rejoicing in each other's company, rejoicing with friends, relishing fine foods, singing songs, with colorful gifts sitting wrapped under the tree. But none of it could ever be because the hard years had come and taken it all away.

Tears began to softly roll from the corners of her eyes, and she thought it odd. She had not cried any tears in a long time. The afternoon passed slowly, but finally, she noticed the sun was starting to set. It was almost time.

As expected, a car pulled up, and a man with neatly combed light brown hair, wearing a gray overcoat, came up the walkway with Aubrey in tow. Matty opened the door and put her plain brown coat on.

Aubrey's dad introduced himself, then Aubrey took Matty by the hand, and they all walked down the freshly shoveled walkway to the waiting car. The car was luxurious, with shiny steel runners and buttons and light blue leather seats. She had never sat in anything so nice.

They pulled onto the road and turned down a crossroad just past the valley, then pulled into the neighborhood on the other side of the field from Matty's old farmhouse. Matty marveled at all the houses they passed, neatly in a row. Most were lit up inside, many with Christmas trees shining in the windows casting the warm glow that seemed to shine brightest on Christmas Eve.

They pulled in the driveway, and Matty clutched her hands together tightly. It was a large house, with lots of rooms up and down. It was white with maroon shutters and a wide blue front door where a beautiful wreath with gold lights glowed brightly. Christmas lights of all colors outlined the front of the structure, and inside, Matty could see a fire and a tall Christmas tree filled with tinsel and bulbs.

Aubrey's father turned off the car and turned to look at Matty in the back seat, announcing, "We are here!"

Matty sighed. Part of her wanted to go back home. She had not been to another house in a very long time, certainly never in one of these modern houses. Her fingers trembled slightly and she felt the moistness forming on the tips of them. She clutched her hands together, trying to calm herself.

Aubrey opened the car door, jumped out, and ran inside, shouting, "Mom, Matty is here."

Aubrey's father then came around and opened the car door for Matty. Matty got out and stood for a moment in the chilly night air. It was already dark outside, but it was more. It was Christmas Eve, indeed. She could feel the old magic in the air. She closed her eyes, drawing in a breath, the smell of the cold fresh air giving her a sense of peace she had not felt in a very long time. She instinctively looked over to her right. There, beneath the light of a full moon, stood Cemetery Hill, with its large barren oaks standing guard, perfectly still in the chilly, crisp night air. Matty had never seen it from this angle, and she thought it looked incredibly beautiful.

"Are you ready, Matty?" Aubrey's father asked, extending his hand to escort her.

"Yes," she replied, but before taking his hand, she looked one more time at the skies above the distant cemetery. She remembered the old story, told every year, and thought to herself. *Angels would be coming soon. Angels would be heard on high, sweetly singing o'er the plains.* She did not know why she thought this, but the skies over Cemetery Hill looked like the perfect scene for such an occurrence.

Matty smiled, took the man's hand, and started for the door.

Chapter 7

They walked down the short sidewalk, up one step, and into the house. Immediately the noise and lights hit her. It had been a very long time since she had been away from quiet and solitude. Lots of people were there. She worried that it would be too much for her. Three or four couples were sitting in the dining room, laughing and talking around a large oak table adorned with food trays. There were children too, a fair number of them, of all ages, running around, laughing and playing noisily.

Matty stayed in the entryway, her fingers clutched against the palm of her hands, feeling afraid to go in. It was the children she was scared of, but no sooner did she observe all this when Aubrey's mother, Colleen, came down the hall, bearing a wide smile and drying her hands with a kitchen towel. Aubrey and Avery were right behind her. "Hi, Matty. Merry Christmas," Colleen warmly said as she extended her hand.

Matty relaxed and took it, saying feebly, "Thank you."

Colleen gestured, "Please, come in. Here, let me take your coat."

Matty handed her coat to Colleen and glanced around at the myriad of colors, her eyes wide, unsure what to do. Inside she felt her heart racing, and her breathing quicken. She glanced over to the door, thinking she needed to leave.

Colleen asked, "Are you OK, Matty?"

She hesitated, looking again around the room. She saw Aubrey across the way handing a cookie from the table to Avery. Matty swallowed her fear, and uttered the words, "Uhhh... yes... I'm... OK."

She pointed to a chair just inside the living room, not far from the door, and asked softly, "May I sit there?"

"Yes, certainly," Colleen replied, as she quickly turned to hang Matty's coat and then ushered her over to the chair.

Aubrey and Avery rushed over and stood in front of Matty, smiling, staring at her, not sure what to say.

Aubrey broke the silence, "Merry Christmas, Matty."

"Yes," Avery said, giddily laughing, "Merry Christmas, Matty."

Matty replied, "Well, Merry Christmas to you, girls." As soon as the words left her mouth, Matty felt a warmth she had not felt in ages. A tear fell from her cheek, and she quickly brushed it away.

Colleen came over and gave her a glass of ginger ale and a small bowl of chips. "Here is a snack, Matty. We will have dinner in a little while."

"Thank you," Matty said as she sat quietly eating, observing everyone, periodically looking out into the night sky, sometimes leaning over to see the moonlit oak trees on top of the cemetery in the distance.

A half hour passed as Matty sat quietly in her chair in the living room, watching Aubrey and Avery playing with the other children. At one point, Colleen called out from the kitchen, "Aubrey, see if Matty needs anything."

In the next instant, Aubrey and Avery came running around the corner, sliding in their socks to a stop on the shiny wooden floor. "Matty, do you need anything?" asked Aubrey.

"No, no, I am just fine. Thank you."

Aubrey nodded, then asked, "Do you have children?"

The question caught Matty off guard. She swallowed and replied in a timid voice, "Oh, uhhh, yes... yes, I do."

"Where are they?"

Matty didn't know what to say. She sighed, knowing the child's innocence in asking, and replied, "They are not far."

"How old are they?" asked Avery this time.

Matty glanced out the window into the night sky and said, "I don't know anymore."

There was a silence between them now, as Matty did not want to say anything else.

Just then, Colleen came down the hall, announcing, "Okay, everyone, dinner is ready. Take your seats." She called out, "Aubrey and Avery, show Matty where her seat is."

Matty was seated near the end of the table closest to the living room. She counted at least twenty people seated. The table had platters of carved ham and roast beef, bowls of mashed potatoes, corn, and beans, along with two baskets of homemade dinner rolls, and several bottles of Vernor's ginger ale and Coca Cola.

Matty enjoyed the meal very much, though she only had a taste of everything. She was not used to eating like this. She tried to keep to herself, as she didn't know what to say. The many questions asked of her were greeted with momentary smiles and one-word answers. Then she would put her head down and quietly resume eating.

After dinner, she returned to her chair by the living room entrance and quietly observed all the children playing. She remembered Christmas Eves past before the hard years had come. In those years, she had imagined her house full of children, running and playing in the excitement that Christmas Eve seemed to uniquely offer. It had been a long time since she had longed for those days, but tonight she found herself longing for them again.

The rest of the night passed quickly for Matty. She had forgotten what it was like to be in a house full of people. Eventually, as Christmas Eve wound its way down, the other couples there packed up their children and left for home.

Chapter 8

Now it was only Matty, with Colleen, her husband, and the two girls. While the others were in the kitchen, Colleen pulled up a chair and said, "Matty, my husband will take you home soon. Are you able to sit and talk for a little while longer? I have been too busy to talk with you."

Although she was tired, Matty was enjoying her evening, so she replied, "I can stay a little longer."

"Oh, good," Colleen said, leaning a little closer. "So, Matty, tell me about yourself."

"Well, there is not much to tell. My husband died, well, a long time ago, 1928, I think."

"Really?" Colleen said. "That was a long time ago."

Matty thought for a moment and asked, "What year is it now?"

Colleen thought it was odd her asking, but she replied, "It's 1953."

"1953?" Matty said, surprised, as her forehead furrowed and her eyebrows lowered. Something was bothering her.

Suddenly Avery ran past, screaming with delight, as Aubrey chased her around the house. Matty sat back, startled, her face growing ashen.

"Girls!" Colleen said sternly, "Stop running."

Colleen waited for them to leave, then looked at Matty, "Matty, I'm sorry. Is everything OK? It looked like they really startled you."

Matty sighed, "I'm ok. Well, you see, I am afraid of children... and I think children are afraid of me too."

Colleen quickly replied, "Oh, now Matty, my girls are not afraid of you. They like you."

Matty nodded slowly, as a flat smile spread across her face, and then a tear fell. "I can see that," she said. "I like them too."

Colleen asked, "Do you have children, Matty?"

Matty shook her head quickly, "I did... but they are gone."

"Where did they go?"

"They all died," Matty replied, her voice trailing away.

Colleen stopped, and her mouth opened, "I'm sorry. How did they die?"

Matty's voice trailed off as she glanced out at the night sky, "Oh, you know... back in those days... children sometimes... " She stumbled to find the words, adding, ….."didn't live very long."

There was a moment of silence, "I'm so sorry, Matty," Colleen said, leaning closer, gently rubbing Matty's forearm.

Matty looked up, her eyes sad, too full to hold anything in. She said, "I really have never told anyone. But... but I... I want you to know." Her eyes were moistening now, as she clutched her hands tightly together, then began.

"When I was twenty-four years old, we had our first baby, named George, but after sixteen days, he stopped breathing one night. He was alone in his crib, and I didn't hear him stop.

That was back in 1887." She glanced toward the window, to the crest of Cemetery Hill, and continued. "It was a cold day, one I will never forget. It was February 12th, Abraham Lincoln's birthday. My husband bought a family plot up there on Cemetery Hill to bury little George."

"A year later, in 1888, we had another baby, a girl this time, and we named her Catherine. But only a month later, she got a fever and… she was sick for four days until the doctor came and said there was nothing we could do. We buried her in the summertime that year, right next to little George."

Matty glanced out the window again, remembering it all. "The following summer was the worst of my life. I almost died giving birth that summer. That happened to women in those days, you know. It was a terribly hot day, and I don't remember much. After the birth, I fell unconscious for seven whole days, and when I finally came too, they told me I had given birth to a little girl. She was badly injured during birthing, you see, and she only lived one day." Matty lowered her head, her lips tight, thinking. "I never even got to see her."

Colleen asked softly, "What was her name?"

"I call her Sarah, but they did not name her because I was unconscious. They called her Baby Korza on her tombstone. Her name, though, is Sarah."

Colleen placed her hand on Matty's forearm, "I am so sorry."

Matty closed her eyes, as a few tears crept out of the corners of them. "I called those the hard years," she said. "My husband George tried to be strong for us, but I was very, very cold toward him after that. I lived in a shell, it seemed. Seven years later, I had another baby, a beautiful boy named Adolph. He survived for a long number of months, and it was the happiest time of our life, but then, in late August of that same year, he got really sick with a fever. Within three days, he was gone. The hard years came back to us. We never had another child. Years later, my husband George died... and ever since then, I have been stuck. I have been afraid of children, and I think that they are afraid of me."

Silence ensued for a few still moments as Matty and Colleen both sat looking up at Cemetery Hill. "I'm so sorry, Matty," Colleen said as she leaned over and gave her a warm hug.

Just then, Aubrey and Avery came running around the corner, laughing and chasing each other. Colleen grabbed them, "Girls, stop running.

"Oh, it's OK," Matty said. She opened her arms and let each girl come to her, and she hugged them both.

Aubrey said, "Thank you for coming, Matty. We love you." Avery rested her head on Matty's shoulder, "Yes, we love you, Matty. Come back."

Matty held them both, one in each arm, and her eyes began to water. She wasn't afraid anymore. She pulled them close, squeezing them, and said, "Thank you, girls."

"Merry Christmas, Matty," Aubrey said. Avery laughed and joined in, "Merry Christmas, Matty."

Colleen asked, "Matty, we have a spare room. Would you like to stay the night?"

Matty thought for a moment. She loved it here, and she loved this little family. It would certainly be pleasant to stay and spend Christmas with them. She glanced out the window into the night sky and remembered the magic of Christmas Eve.

It was still out there.

She leaned forward, taking in the view of Cemetery Hill. It looked alive tonight, full of wonder. She turned to Colleen, smiling, and said, "No, thank you. I think I am ready to go home now."

"OK, Matty," Colleen said tenderly. She then said more firmly, "Go get your father, girls."

She helped Matty to stand up, then hugged her warmly and said, "Merry Christmas, Matty."

Matty smiled, repeating her reply from earlier, "Yes, I... I think it is time to go home."

Chapter 9

A little while later, Aubrey's father helped Matty out of the car and helped her up the walk and stairs. He opened the door and asked, "Can I help you get inside?"

"No," Matty replied, "but thank you for everything." She stepped inside the dark house, closed the door, and crossed the living room floor, heading for the stairs. It was never dark when she went to bed, and it was more difficult to find her way, but it didn't matter tonight.

Nothing mattered tonight.

~ ~ ~ ~

The following morning, Matty opened her eyes, aware that it was Christmas Day for the first time in ages. She was quiet for a long time, thinking about the little girls, Aubrey and Avery, and the kindness that had been shown her. Then, she heard the old familiar voice.

It was the man. "Matty, wake up."

Matty looked over at him. Her eyes were not tired this morning. They felt young and strong and full of hope. She was glad he was there, and for the first time in a very long time, she was happy to see him.

In a tender tone, the man asked, "Are you ready to go home, Matty?"

She sighed heavily and replied, "I think so…. I think I'm ready now."

~ ~ ~ ~

The following day, after breakfast and after opening all the gifts, Colleen turned to her husband and said, "I'm going to bring Matty a plate of food. Aubrey, do you want to come with me?"

"Yes, Mommy," Aubrey replied.

Colleen smiled and said, "OK, go, get dressed. Avery, you stay here with dad."

They fixed up a plate and drove over to Matty's house on the other side of the farmland field. Colleen and Aubrey went up the snow-filled walk, up the snow-filled steps, to the door, and knocked. The house looked more beaten and worn than it had the day before. The gutter was loose on the far end of the porch, and Colleen noticed the front window had a large crack running across it.

She knocked again.

While she waited, she looked back at the walkway. She and Aubrey's footsteps were freshly imprinted in the snow. She looked at the other walks nearby. They were all cleanly shoveled. It had not snowed in days. Colleen looked down at Aubrey and remarked, "I could have sworn the walk was shoveled when we came a few days ago."

She knocked again. There was no answer. She peeked inside and saw the basket she had given Matty days earlier, untouched, sitting on the end table with the nut bread still inside. "Hmmm," Colleen said, "She must be asleep."

They walked back to their car.

The next-door neighbor was out shoveling his drive. Colleen put Aubrey into the car's front seat, closed the door, and went up to the man. She asked, "Have you seen Matty today?"

The man looked at her, perplexed, "Who?"

Colleen turned and pointed to the house. "Matty. She lives there."

The man replied, "Lady, that house has been empty for almost ten years now."

"No, you don't understand. I just spoke to her yesterday."

The man's face bore confusion for a moment. He said, "I am not sure who you mean, but that lady died a long time ago." He turned to the cemetery. "Her family's gravestone is up there on Cemetery Hill. I know, because it is right near my parents' gravestone."

Colleen's heart began racing, as she glanced across the valley to the cemetery. She turned back to the man, and asked, "W...w...where is it?"

He pointed and replied, "Right when you get to the top, and you turn right onto the perimeter road. It is the first gravestone on the right, a large red granite one."

Colleen went back to the car and got in with her hands shaking. Aubrey looked at her and asked, "Is everything OK, mom?"

"Yes, yes, everything is fine. I just have to go look at something." She put the car in drive and headed to the cemetery entrance, and slowly drove up the winding, zig-zag road that led to the plateau of Cemetery Hill. She turned right onto the perimeter road as the man had directed her, then stopped.

"What are we doing here, mom?" Aubrey asked.

Colleen replied, "Wait here for a minute."

Colleen got out and walked to the large red granite gravestone. There on the stone, prominently displayed, was the family name. It read KORZA. She stepped up closer and nervously scanned the stone, trying to take it all in as quickly as she could. Below the family name, KORZA, the first names were listed.

The first line said Husband - George.

The next line read Wife - Elizabeth, lovingly known as "Matty."

The next four lines listed the four children. All the names and dates, just as Matty had said.

Colleen's eyes darted quickly back up to Matty's name. Next to it was her date of death, 1942.

It was eleven years ago.

Colleen began to tremble, and her heart began to race. She thought back to the night before, to her conversation, to Matty's story, her tears, her warm hug. Colleen looked up at the barren oak trees, swaying gently in the Christmas morning breeze, trying to understand.

Then, she saw a piece of paper, neatly folded under a small rock, sitting on top of the red granite gravestone. She hesitantly took it and unfolded it. It read, "Dear Colleen, Aubrey, and Avery. Thank you for helping me. I am going home now."

Colleen trembled more, closing her eyes, trying to calm her fears, thinking about Matty's words from the night before "Ever since then, I have been stuck... No, I am ready to go home now."

A small tear fell from Colleen's eye as she looked up into the clouds... and she somehow understood.

Suddenly a brisk wind rushed through the cemetery, and the paper flew out of her hand. She tried to grab it, but it flew up, twirling in the sky. Colleen watched it, hoping it would come down, but it just kept ascending like a balloon and disappeared into the clouds.

She thought once more of the warm hug Matty had given her, and of her tears, and of her smile as she left last night. She thought of Matty's final words again, "It is time for me to go home."

Colleen wiped the tears, forming faster now in her eyes. She wasn't sure what to do or say, but she was glad.

They had helped Matty.

Chapter 10

Matty suddenly found herself standing in front of a white house with freshly painted green shutters and a large wreath on the door. It was snowing, but she was not cold. A man approached her. It was the man who had visited her often and who took care of her sidewalks, cleaning off the snow for her. His face was bright today and adorned with a cheerful smile.

He said, "Good morning, Matty."

"Good morning to you," she said, as she glanced up at the house, then back at him. She asked, "Is this my house?"

"Yes, it is," he said and pointed, "Look over there. There is the hill the children used to sled down and look beyond. There is the hill where the cemetery was."

Matty turned and looked up at Cemetery Hill. It was standing as proud as ever, with its oak trees majestically adorning the perimeter, their barren branches swaying in the winter wind, but they were different. The branches, though barren, seemed alive and full of hope. Then she noticed something else. All the gravestones were gone. All that was on the hill was snow and a road that circled the plateau. Matty turned to the man, her eyebrows drawn together, feeling suddenly anxious. She asked, "Where are the graves?"

The man replied, "There are no graves here, Matty. We don't need them."

Matty's mouth opened wide as she slowly began to nod. She understood.

She turned and looked back up at the house. The lights were on inside, giving off a warm glow Matty had not seen in a very long time. She looked at the man again, her eyes sagging some as if she was afraid. "Who is in there?" she asked.

"George is inside, Matty," the man said gently, "and so are the children."

Matty's eyes watered as she looked up. She clutched the man's arm and said, "I don't know if I'm ready."

The man reassured her, "I understand, Matty. You were not ready before, but I think you may be now."

Matty's face grew sullen, and she lamented, "But I was supposed to keep them safe."

The man replied as warmly as he could, "Matty, it wasn't your fault. I told you... they are all doing well. They are waiting for you."

Matty thought about what he said. Her chin lowered to her chest, and she closed her eyes tightly and said softly, "I think I'm ready. I'm not afraid anymore."

The man smiled and waited for her to take the first step. She looked up at the warm glow coming from inside the house again and sighed heavily, letting the last of her fear all out. She looked up at the man, her eyes narrowed some, and asked in a questioning tone, "Are you a ghost?"

The man replied, "No."

"Then, who are you?" Matty asked.

"I am your Angel."

Matty's eyes began to twinkle, "You are, are you? Well, why didn't you say so?"

The man started laughing and extended his hand. "Are you ready, Matty?"

"Yes," she said, as she took his hand, and they walked up to the door together. The man knocked, then opened the door and announced, "George, you have a visitor."

In a moment, George rounded the corner looking as handsome as Matty ever remembered. He was young and strong, and his black hair and smiling blue eyes looked just like the day she had first met him. "Matty!" he exclaimed.

"Oh, George," Matty said as she stepped into his arms and hugged him tightly, tears running down her face. They kissed for a long time, then pulled apart to look at each other.

"You look so beautiful, Matty," he said.

Matty glanced in the full-length mirror next to the entrance closet. She was still wearing her blue flowered dress, but her hair was brown again, and curly, and her eyes were dark brown, alive with the glow of life. Her lips were red, and her face smooth. She was young again. She lifted her foot and saw that her legs were muscular and slim. She twirled her ankle, watching her white shoe twirl as it once used to. She looked into George's eyes, asking, "George is it all real?"

"Yes, it is. We've been waiting for you." He took her by the hand and led her into the front room. A fire was going in the fireplace, and a Christmas tree was in the corner, full of lights and decorations. George called out, "Children, Mom is home."

Suddenly, a boy who looked to be about four came bounding around the corner, followed immediately by a girl, a year younger, then another girl followed, younger than the first. Matty dropped to her knees, and they all rushed into her arms, crying out, "Mom!" They hugged her tightly, resting their heads against her shoulder, jostling to get close.

Matty's face beamed with joy as she hugged them, kissing them, her tears flowing freely. Just then, another boy, a toddler, came waddling around the corner, barreling recklessly into the group.

"Oh, look," Matty said, pulling him in. "Oh, my beautiful children," she cried. She took them all into her arms again, hugging and kissing them as they laughed and giggled. Matty looked up at George, her face wet with tears, and exclaimed, "George, our children... they are here with us."

"Yes, they are, Matty. Welcome, home, darling. And Merry Christmas."

~ ~ ~ ~

Outside, the man stood on the sidewalk, looking up at the farmhouse, smiling. Matty had made it, and they were a family again. She and George would have their chance to raise the children now as they had always longed to do.

His work here was finished. He flew up into the air and headed for home.

The end? No, it's only the beginning.

The Story of The Ghost of Christmas to Come

I was attending the wedding of my wife's cousin, Danielle, at a church in the southern suburbs of Cleveland, Ohio. I had forgotten to walk in with my face mask, so I went out to the car and noticed an old cemetery, seemingly forgotten by time, tucked away in the back of the grounds.

I went in, looking at the old graves, and suddenly found the most interesting gravestone. A husband and wife were listed, both born during the Civil War. He had died about 12 years before her. There were four other names on the monument: all children, all listed as having died in the same year they were born. Nearby were smaller headstones for the children, listing exact dates of birth and death.

I thought of how hard this must have been for the mother and the father, but especially the mother. Since I had planned on attempting to write my second Christmas story this year, following my first one written last year, called *Starry Night*, I thought of a story and decided to call it, *The Ghost of Christmas to Come*. Why named? Because of the influence of Charles Dickens, of course, the author of *A Christmas Carol*, and the subject of the movie *The Man Who Invented Christmas*. This story, like his classic, is a tale of redemption, not regret.

Matty's Gravestone

Final Things
Could you rate this book with on Amazon?

Review on Amazon
To find me on amazon, search DP Conway books.

Sign Up for my Monthly Newsletter at
dpconway.com
I promise not to annoy you.

Drawing from his Irish American heritage, D.P. Conway weaves faith and hope into his storytelling, exploring the profound mysteries of life and its connection to the Angels and the rest of the unseen Eternal World. His works consistently convey the triumph of light over darkness, inspiring readers to find strength and solace amidst life's trials.

Also by D. P. Conway

Stand Alone Novels
Las Vegas Down
Parkland
The Wancheen
Marisella

The Christmas Collection
Starry Night
The Ghost of Christmas to Come
Nava
Twelve Days
Home for Christmas

Coming Soon
Mary Queen of Hearts
And hopefully many, many, more….

Afterlife Chronicles: Angel Sagas Series
The Epic Series based on Genesis and Revelation
Dawn of Days
Rebellion
Judgment
Empire
The Innocents
And 7 more titles in this epic series.

See many more of D.P. Conway's books on Amazon or visit
www.dpconway.com

Copyright & Publication

Daylights Publishing
5498 Dorothy Drive Suite 3:16
Cleveland, OH 44070

www.dpconway.com
www.daylightspublishing.com

Photo sources and credits are listed at www.dpconway.com

Cover: Nate Myers Colleen Conway Cooper
Developmental Editor: Colleen Conway Cooper
Editor: Connie Swenson

Made in the USA
Middletown, DE
21 December 2023

46510344R00035